Traxler

JUV/E   Cote, Nancy.
FIC

Palm trees.

$14.95

DATE			

PALM TREES

by Nancy Cote

Four Winds Press ✳ New York

Maxwell Macmillan Canada   Toronto

Maxwell Macmillan International   New York   Oxford   Singapore   Sydney

The morning sun rose over the city rooftops. Silent, giant shadows grew on the sidewalks and streets below. From her bedroom window, Millie watched her mother leave for work. The hot August air felt heavy with dampness.

That's why Millie knew that today she would have trouble fixing her hair. Millie looked into the mirror. Her hair seemed twice as big as usual. It was very hard to comb. Brushing only made it larger.

Like her dad's tight curls, Millie's hair was thick enough for two. She wished it could be like her mom's soft brown waves.

Millie's hair stuck out like an old broken umbrella, and she wished her mom was home to fix it. Momma had a way of tying it back or braiding it so that it always looked nice. Now that her mom was working, Millie would have to do this by herself. It would not be easy.

After making a nice, even part in her hair, Millie lifted one side and tied it with a rubber band. Her hands were clumsy. Tying up the next side was easier. It was cooler with her hair off her neck.

Millie felt proud. She smiled a wide smile into the mirror and looked in her closet for an outfit that would make her feel grown-up. She decided on her striped jumper because it would spin very nicely. Slipping on her black leather shoes, she gave a twirl and *click-clacked* out the door to meet her friend Renee.

Although it was very hot, Millie skipped at a quick pace. In the distance she spotted Renee's flowing blue ribbons, and she ran to join her.

"My gosh," laughed Renee as she walked toward Millie. "You've got palm trees on top of your head."

Millie's cheeks burned. She felt foolish and turned to run home. Everyone she passed seemed to be staring at her.

Getting home took forever. The sun was high in the sky, and it cast Millie's shadow on the sidewalk in front of her. The image of palm trees dancing before her all the way home convinced Millie that she looked silly.

Millie ran into her building. She raced upstairs and into her mother's empty bedroom. She jumped onto her mom's empty bed and squeezed her eyes shut tight. How she longed for her mother's hug and to be told everything was all right.

When Millie opened her eyes, she spotted her mom's open sewing box. There in the box was a pair of shiny scissors.

"Maybe if I cut my hair I would look better," Millie whispered.

But thoughts of braids and ribbons and hair on her shoulders ran through Millie's mind. Then her face began to feel warm again as the memory of Renee's laughter returned.

Millie pulled at one curl and slowly lifted the scissors.
She closed her eyes and opened the scissors wide. . . .
    Just then there was a knock at the door. Millie let out
a deep breath and ran to answer it.

She opened the door and there stood Renee. She had palm trees, three of them, on the top of her head. Millie and Renee exploded with laughter at the sight of each other and their identical hair.

Their laughter made the palm trees jiggle...and the jiggling made the girls laugh even harder. They were laughing so hard they couldn't speak. Above the city noises rang the sound of friendship...a sound more powerful than the beating summer sun.

The day passed quickly, and Millie and Renee had more fun than they had ever had before. They fixed pigtails and elephant ears and parakeet toes, finally finishing with a plop-on-top.

"Hey, none of these is as cool as your trees," said Renee. And once again five swaying palm trees appeared on the heads of the two good friends.

The evening sun filled the apartment with a golden color. Millie felt golden on the inside, too.

Perching on the rooftops, the sun glowed once more in Millie's direction, then drifted down slowly, leaving a cool, blue night sky.

Millie's hair was still twice as big as usual, but so was her smile, and she felt very happy.

Millie's mother arrived home from work. She took a good, long look at the girls. With a smile and a shake of her head she said, "My, my, you two are growing like trees!"

All at once Millie and Renee burst into laughter again. "Palm trees, Momma, palm trees!"

To Mike, for all his support
Katie, her strength
John, his kisses
and Missy, the inspiration